DATE DUE

MAR 2 8 2004		

Demco

PETER PENNY'S DANCE

PETER PENNY'S DANCE

by **Janet Quin-Harkin** / *pictures by* **Anita Lobel**

THE DIAL PRESS, NEW YORK

Text copyright © 1976 by Janet Quin-Harkin
Pictures copyright © 1976 by Anita Lobel
All rights reserved / First Printing
Printed in the United States of America
by Holyoke Lithograph Co.
Bound by Economy Bookbinding Corporation
Warren Wallerstein, Director of Production
Typography by Atha Tehon

Library of Congress Cataloging in Publication Data
Quin-Harkin, Janet. Peter Penny's dance.
1. Voyages around the world—Fiction]
I. Lobel, Anita. II. Title.
PZ7.Q419Pe [E] 75-27600
ISBN 0-8037-7183-5 ISBN 0-8037-7184-3 lib. bdg.

For Clare, Anne, Jane, and Dominic

Long ago on a ship of the King's Navy there lived a sailor named Peter Penny, who could dance the sailor's hornpipe better than any other man. He danced on the deck when he should have been scrubbing. He danced in the galley when he should have been cooking. He danced in the crow's nest when he should have been looking.

The captain of the ship grew very angry. "Peter Penny," he said, "you are no use as a sailor. All you like to do is dance. You must leave my ship."

"Very well," said Peter Penny. "I shall leave the navy. I shall dance 'round the world."

The captain laughed. "Nobody could dance all the way around the world," he said.

"I can," said Peter Penny.

The captain kept on laughing. "I'll wager one golden guinea that you can't."

Peter Penny thought a little. Then he said, "Captain, a golden guinea is no use to me, for I hope to make my fortune as I dance. But I should like to marry your daughter when I return."

The captain knew his daughter wanted to marry Peter Penny. "If you can dance around the world," he said, "Lavinia will marry you. But hurry back, Peter Penny. Lavinia is pretty and clever, you know, and she will only wait five years for you." He thought it was impossible for Peter to return so soon. His daughter would forget all about the penniless sailor, and he could persuade her to marry a rich merchant.

Peter packed up his bundle and got ready to start. Lavinia was sad to see him go. "Take care now, Peter Penny," she said. "I've drawn you a map of the world, made you some nice cold beef sandwiches in case you get hungry, and here's an apple to put in your pocket."

Peter waved to Lavinia and set off. He danced down to the harbor and right onto a ship leaving for France. He danced off again in a French town.

The people in France had never seen such a good dancer as Peter Penny. They told their cousins about him, and the cousins told their cousins too. Peter became famous. When he danced into a town, people lined the streets to watch and cheer, the town band played, and the mayor read a speech. Sometimes the speech was so long that Peter had already danced out of the town before it was over.

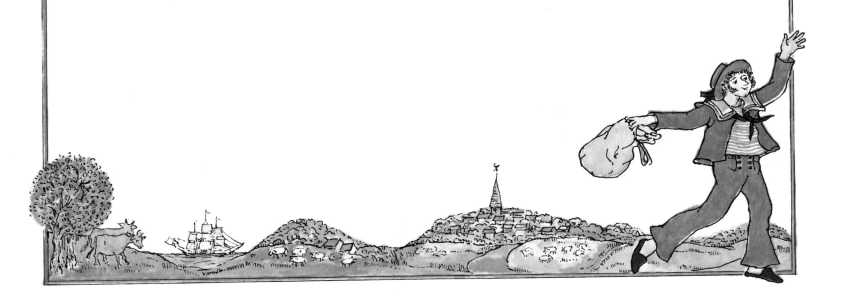

Soon even the king of France heard about Peter Penny. He rode out in his golden coach with all the little princesses and the little prince and asked Peter to become the Royal Dancing Master. Peter thanked him kindly and said that he was sorry but he couldn't stay because he was dancing 'round the world.

Then the king gave Peter a bag of gold and jewels and two dozen frog's legs, which people in France like to eat.

Peter set off again. When he came to some hills at the bottom of France, he danced right over them into Spain.

Soon he came to a bullring, where a large crowd was gathered to watch a matador fight a fierce bull. Peter wanted to show the crowd how well he could dance, so he danced all the way around the ring. The bull chased him, but he danced so fast that finally the bull got tired and fell asleep.

"*Olé! Olé!*" cried all the people, which means "Well done." They wanted to make Peter the head matador. But Peter danced out of the bullring and away through Spain. He didn't like bulls very much.

At the bottom of Spain he found a sea. He danced onto a ship that was sailing to Africa. On the other side of the sea he danced off again. The land at the top of Africa was a dry, sandy desert that burned his feet.

Peter looked at his map, but there were no roads or signposts, and he would have lost his way if he hadn't followed a friendly camel. There was no water to drink in the desert. After a few days he began to feel very thirsty. Then Peter remembered the apple in his pocket. So he ate that, and soon he felt fine again.

At last the great desert came to an end. Before Peter stretched wide grasslands full of all kinds of animals. Peter had never seen giraffes and zebras, antelopes and monkeys before, and the animals had never seen anything as strange as Peter Penny. They stopped what they were doing and followed him. Even the lions stopped hunting their dinner and followed Peter Penny's dance. Soon Peter had a whole line of animals trotting behind him.

Now on those same grasslands lived proud Masai warriors. They were holding their secret hunting dance when Peter Penny danced right into their midst.

"A stranger has come into our magic hunting dance," they cried. "He must die!"

They raised their long spears, and things looked very bad for Peter Penny. Then the warriors saw all the animals. "This man must have powerful magic," they said. "Even the lions follow him." So they invited Peter to their feast.

Afterward he wished the warriors good luck and set off again, followed by his procession of animals. At a small seaport he was just in time to catch an Arabian ship that was sailing for India.

India was full of elephants and beautiful temples. In the temples were dancers who could wiggle their heads from side to side. They were very pleased to see Peter. "What a good dancer," they said. "Why don't you stay and dance in the temple with us?"

"Thanks very much, but I'm dancing 'round the world," said Peter. "And anyway, I can't wiggle my head."

He danced out of India and over the mountains to China. Around China was the Great Wall, the longest wall in the world. Peter danced right up to it, and then he danced right over it.

"Someone has just danced over our wall," said one of the fierce soldiers who guarded it. "We must take him to the emperor."

So they took Peter to the palace of the emperor of China. The emperor looked at Peter and frowned. "The law of China says that anyone who climbs over the Great Wall must die," he said.

"But this man *danced* over the wall," said the empress. "The law doesn't say anything about dancing."

"Very well, Peter Penny," said the emperor. "Let us see you dance. If you can dance all around my palace, past the three thousand waterfalls and the four thousand bridges and the five thousand gates and the six thousand courtyards and return before the sun sets, you shall go free. If you cannot, you shall die."

Peter was pleased to show the emperor how well he could dance. He danced past the waterfalls and bridges, the gates and courtyards and was back in time for tea.

The emperor was amazed. He asked Peter to stay on at the palace. But he had promised Peter he could go free. So he gave him a bag of gold and jewels and a gallon of bird's nest soup.

Peter danced out of the palace and kept on dancing until he came to another sea. The harbor was full of Chinese boats called junks. Peter found the biggest and best junk in the harbor. Its owner's name was Li Wong. Peter asked Li Wong if he would like to sail across the ocean in search of adventure. Li Wong said he would, so they set out the next day.

Halfway across the ocean they were caught in a typhoon. The wind howled, and the waves were as high as a house. Li Wong's junk was tossed up and down.

At last it was washed up on the shores of a tropical island where a dozen lovely girls were dancing the hula. Peter knew from his map that the island was Hawaii. When the girls saw Peter Penny dance, they asked him to stay. Peter wanted to stay and dance the hula, but Li Wong reminded him about the captain's daughter, and Peter knew that he must make his way home. The girls filled the junk with pineapples, and Peter and Li Wong sailed away.

After many weeks at sea, when they were down to their last slice of pineapple, they saw a steep, rocky coast. It was California. Peter said good-bye to his friend Li Wong, giving him the biggest jewel and one bag of gold as a present.

Then Peter set out to dance across America. He danced across a desert, then over some high mountains. On the other side of the mountains he came upon a buffalo herd. When the buffalo saw Peter, they became very frightened and started to run. But Peter danced right behind them. Faster and faster they went, but they couldn't run away from Peter Penny. At last the buffalo came to a cliff and fell down into the valley below.

The Indians living in that valley were amazed to see meat for the whole winter come falling from the sky. When they learned that Peter Penny had hunted the buffalo, they prepared a huge feast in his honor. They asked him to stay and become a brave of the tribe. Peter thanked them kindly but said he was dancing 'round the world. So they gave him plenty of buffalo stew, and he danced away.

It took Peter many weeks to cross America. He saw no other people, but sometimes Indian scouts saw him. They could tell he was friendly so they didn't stop him from dancing.

Peter became very lonely and very hungry. He had eaten all the buffalo stew and he had to make do with wild corn and berries. With no proper food he danced more and more slowly. Summer turned to winter and he danced through the first snowfall. He grew cold and tired. He thought his dance had come to an end, and nobody in the world would ever hear about it.

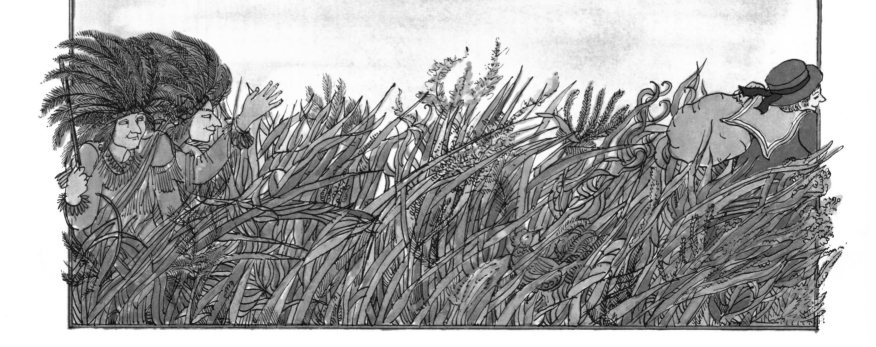

Just when he could go no farther, he smelled a most delicious smell. Roast turkey! His nose led him to a neat little wooden town. Out of every house came the same mouthwatering smell. Peter had arrived in time for Thanksgiving.

The people in the town invited Peter to share their feast with them. After dinner he felt stronger right away and did a special Thanksgiving dance for them. When it was time to leave, they gave him plenty of cold turkey and pumpkin pie and showed him the way to the harbor where a ship would sail for England.

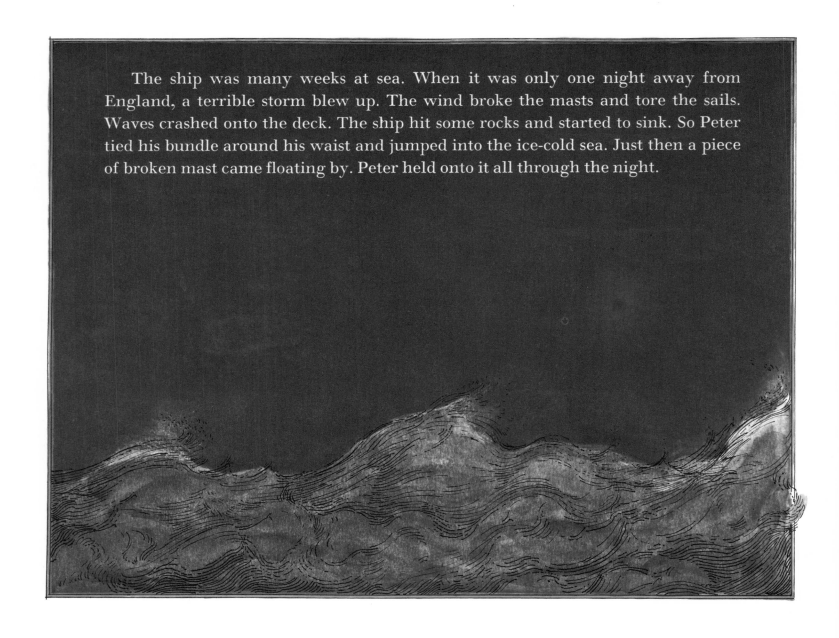

The ship was many weeks at sea. When it was only one night away from England, a terrible storm blew up. The wind broke the masts and tore the sails. Waves crashed onto the deck. The ship hit some rocks and started to sink. So Peter tied his bundle around his waist and jumped into the ice-cold sea. Just then a piece of broken mast came floating by. Peter held onto it all through the night.

Just when he felt he couldn't hold on for another moment, the storm died down, the sun came up, and he could see the coast of England.

He swam ashore and found by looking at his map that he had landed only a few miles from his own town. So he emptied the sea water out of his shoes and set off, leaving a trail of drips behind him.

As he danced into the square, he saw a large crowd of people.

"What is happening?" he asked.

"Why, it's a wedding," said the man. "Mr. Marchbanks, the rich tea merchant, is marrying the captain's daughter."

"Oh, no, he's not," said Peter Penny, and he danced right into the church and up to Lavinia.

"Thank you, but I've come to claim my bride now," he told the fat merchant.

"We thought you were lost, Peter Penny," said the captain.

"My five years are not up for two more days," said Peter Penny.

"What is going on?" asked the minister.

"I should like to marry Lavinia," said Peter Penny, "if she still wants me."

"Oh, yes," said Lavinia, "but please change your wet clothes first."

So Peter married the captain's daughter. With the gold and jewels in his bundle he bought an elegant coach to ride in and a fine house on a hill with a cook and a gardener. Lavinia still made all the beef sandwiches herself though, and they lived happily for the rest of their days.